Helen Recorvits • Pictures by Gabi Swiatkowska

My Name Is Yoon

SQUARE
FISH

Farrar Straus Giroux
New York

Imprints of Macmillan
175 Fifth Avenue, New York, New York 10010
mackids.com

Square Fish books may be purchased for business or promotional use. For information on bulk purchases,
please contact the Macmillan Corporate and Premium Sales Department at
(800) 221-7945 x5442 or by e-mail at specialmarkets@macmillan.com.

Library of Congress Cataloging-in-Publication Data
Recorvits, Helen.
My name is Yoon / Helen Recorvits ; pictures by Gabi Swiatkowska.
p.   cm.
Summary: Disliking her name as written in English, Korean-born Yoon, or "shining wisdom," refers to herself
as "cat," "bird," and "cupcake," as a way to feel more comfortable in her new school and new country.
1. Korean Americans—Juvenile fiction. [1. Korean Americans—Fiction. 2. Emigration and immigration—Fiction. 3. First
day of school—Fiction. 4. Schools—Fiction.] I. Swiatkwska, Gabriela, ill. II. Title.
PZ7.R24435 My 2003   [E]—dc21   00-51395

Originally published in the United States by Frances Foster Books / Farrar Straus Giroux
First Square Fish Edition: 2014
Book designed by Jennifer Crilly / Square Fish logo designed by Filomena Tuosto

ISBN 978-0-374-35114-4 (FSG hardcover)
19 20

ISBN 978-1-250-05711-2 (Square Fish paperback)
7 9 10 8 6

AR: 2.3 / LEXILE: 320L

For Yoon —H.R.

To Lidia and Michael —G.S.

My name is Yoon. I came here from Korea, a country far away.

It was not long after we settled in that my father called me to his side.

"Soon you will go to your new school. You must learn to print your name in English," he said. "Here. This is how it looks."

I wrinkled my nose. I did not like YOON. Lines. Circles. Each standing alone.

"My name looks happy in Korean," I said. "The symbols dance together.

"And in Korean my name means Shining Wisdom. I like the Korean way better."

"Well, you must learn to write it this way. Remember, even when you write in English, it still means Shining Wisdom."

I did not want to learn the new way. I wanted to go back home to Korea. I did not like America. Everything was different here. But my father handed me a pencil, and his eyes said Do-as-I-say. He showed me how to print every letter in the English alphabet. So I practiced, and my father was very pleased.

"Look," he called to my mother. "See how well our little Yoon does!"

"Yes," she said. "She will be a wonderful student!"

I wrinkled my nose.

My first day at school I sat quietly at my desk while the teacher talked about CAT. She wrote CAT on the chalkboard. She read a story about CAT. I did not know what her words meant, but I knew what the pictures said. She sang a song about CAT. It was a pretty song, and I tried to sing the words, too.

Later she gave me a paper with my name on it.

"Name. Yoon," she said. And she pointed to the empty lines underneath.

I did not want to write YOON. I wrote CAT instead. I wrote CAT on every line.

CAT CAT CAT

I wanted to be CAT. I wanted to hide in a corner.
My mother would find me and cuddle up close to me.
I would close my eyes and mew quietly.

The teacher looked at my paper. She shook her head and frowned. "So you are CAT?" she asked.

The ponytail girl sitting behind me giggled.

After school I said to my father, "We should go back to Korea. It is better there."

"Do not talk like that," he said. "America is your home now."

I sat by the window and watched a little robin hop, hop in the yard. "He is all alone, too," I thought. "He has no friends. No one likes him."

Then I had a very good idea. "If I draw a picture for the teacher, then maybe she will like me."

It was the best bird I had ever drawn. "Look, Father," I said proudly.

"Oh, this makes me happy," he said. "Now do this." And he showed me how to print BIRD under the picture.

The next day at school the teacher handed me another YOON paper to print. But I did not want to print YOON. I wrote BIRD instead. I wrote BIRD on every line.

I wanted to be BIRD. I wanted to fly, fly back to Korea. I would fly to my nest, and I would tuck my head under my little brown wing.

The teacher looked at my paper. Again she shook her head. "So you are BIRD?" she asked.

Then I showed her my special robin drawing. I patted my red dress, and then I patted the red robin. I lowered my head and peeked up at her. The teacher smiled.

"How was school today, my daughter?" my mother asked.

"I think the teacher likes me a little," I said.

"Well, that is good!" my mother said.

"Yes, but at my school in Korea, I was my teacher's favorite. I had many friends. Here I am all alone."

"You must be patient with everyone, including yourself," my mother said. "You will be a fine student, and you will make many new friends here."

The next day at recess, I stood near the fence by myself. I watched the ponytail girl sitting on the swing. She watched me, too. Suddenly she jumped off the swing and ran over to me. She had a package in her hand. The wrapper said CUPCAKE. She opened it and gave me one. She giggled. I giggled, too.

When we were back in school, the teacher gave us more printing papers. I did not want to write YOON. I wrote CUPCAKE instead.

I wanted to be CUPCAKE. The children would clap their hands when they saw me. They would be excited. "CUPCAKE!" they would say. "Here is CUPCAKE!"

The teacher looked at my paper. "And today you are CUPCAKE!" she said. She smiled a very big smile. Her eyes said I-like-this-girl-Yoon.

After school I told my mother about my ponytail friend. I sang a new song for my father. I sang in English.

"You make us so proud, little Yoon," my mother said.

"Maybe America will be a good home," I thought. "Maybe different is good, too."

The next day at school, I could hardly wait to print. And this time I wrote YOON on every line.

When my teacher looked at my paper, she gave me a big hug. "Aha! You are YOON!" she said.

Yes, I am YOON.

I write my name in English now. It still means Shining Wisdom.